Don't Be a Schwoe

EMBRACING DIFFERENCES

Barbara E. Mauzy

Schiffer Publishing Ltd

4880 Lower Valley Road, Atglen, Pennsylvania 19310

Schiffer Books are available at special discounts for bulk purchases for sales promotions or premiums. Special editions, including personalized covers, corporate imprints, and excerpts can be created in large quantities for special needs. For more information contact the publisher:

Published by Schiffer Publishing Ltd.
4880 Lower Valley Road
Atglen, PA 19310
Phone: (610) 593-1777; Fax: (610) 593-2002
E-mail: Info@schifferbooks.com

For the largest selection of fine reference books on this and related subjects, please visit our website at **www.schifferbooks.com**
We are always looking for people to write books on new and related subjects. If you have an idea for a book please contact us at the above address.

This book may be purchased from the publisher.
Include $5.00 for shipping.
Please try your bookstore first.
You may write for a free catalog.

In Europe, Schiffer books are distributed by
Bushwood Books
6 Marksbury Ave.
Kew Gardens
Surrey TW9 4JF England
Phone: 44 (0) 20 8392 8585;
Fax: 44 (0) 20 8392 9876
E-mail: info@bushwoodbooks.co.uk
Website: www.bushwoodbooks.co.uk

Dedication

For my grandchildren: Kendyl, Jordan, and Michael, with lots and lots of love.

There is a land far, far away
That takes a week plus one more day
To find beyond the pirate's cay.

I've not been there, but I know
That to get there you need to go
Passed the giant pink plateau.

The land of Par-zee-no.
Just hop aboard a gracious crow
Because he knows the way to go.

You haven't heard of Par-zee-no,
The place where gentle, warm winds blow?
It is home to the elusive Schwoe.

The Schwoe is like you or I —
Eating brussel sprouts on pumpkin pie
And pickle juice on burnt French fries.

Schwoes are the same as you, indeed,
Eating liver ice-cream with seaweed
And a touch of sauerkraut, jellied.

Well, the Schwoe is almost like you.
With arms and legs numbered two
And thumbs to help with all he'll do.

Like kids, some Schwoes are short
 and some are tall,
And some Schwoes can be extremely
 small.
Schwoes can be skinny or shaped
 like a ball.

They like to play and have tons of fun
And waste time when there's work to be done.
Yes, a Schwoe is just like everyone.

Everyone indeed. One Schwoe
Is like any other, if you look to and fro.
They're purple, always purple, don't you know?

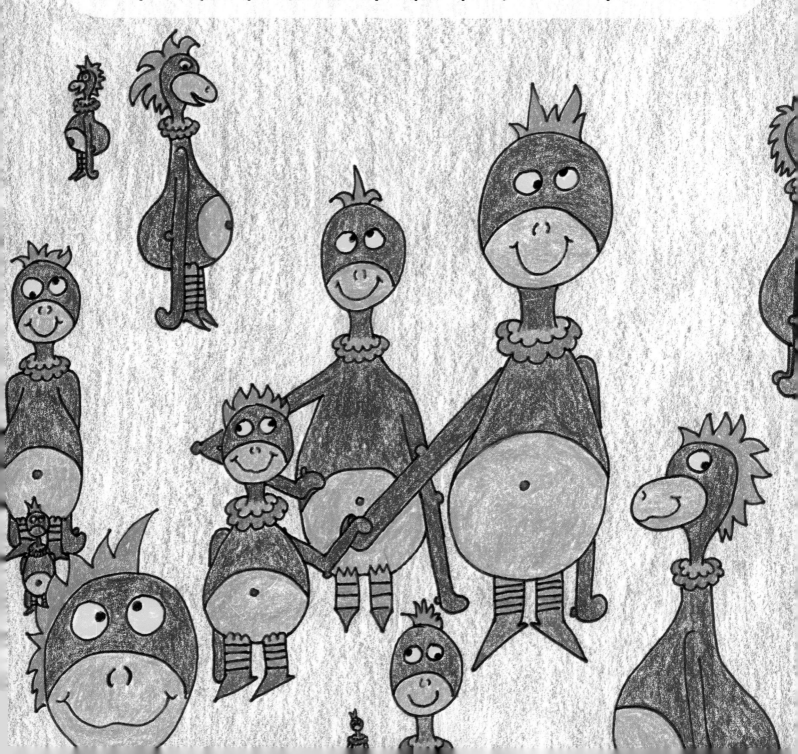

So imagine the surprise there was,
When a baby arrived with ruby fuzz.
Yes, Par-zee-no was all a-buzz.

It made no sense, it caused concern.
Ruby fur – like severe sunburn.
Why? Why? Who could discern?

One thing for certain and for sure:
Schwoe Mommy and Daddy
had much to endure
Raising a Schwoe that was
red to the core.

When taking baby for a walk
Schwoes would gasp, stare, and talk,
Whisper, make jokes, and gawk.

Mommy and Daddy Schwoe
Didn't know where to go
Where hurtful things wouldn't overflow.

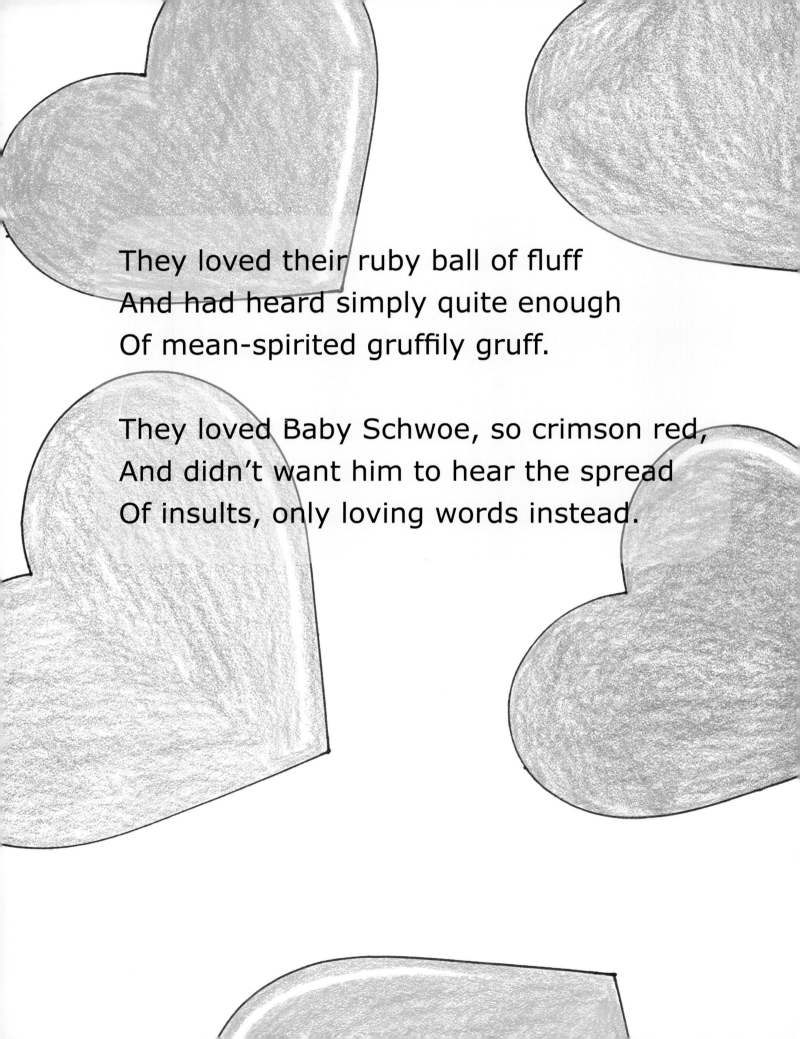

They loved their ruby ball of fluff
And had heard simply quite enough
Of mean-spirited gruffily gruff.

They loved Baby Schwoe, so crimson red,
And didn't want him to hear the spread
Of insults, only loving words instead.

They kept the child in their home
And raised him inside all alone,
Careful to never let him roam.

But time passes, as you know.
Before long to school he had to go...
The one and only ruby Schwoe.

ix 6   seven 7 eight 8   nine 9   ten 10

As he walked inside to find a chair
Schwoes pointed and yelled, "Look over there!"
They ogled at his flaming red hair.

They mocked and jeered and stared so
Just because he was a ruby Schwoe.
He felt so bad, the little fellow.

Mean things were said.
The ridicule was widespread.
He felt embarrassment and dread.

He was confused, hurt, and feeling bad.
He felt totally, terribly, utterly sad.
It was the worst day he'd ever had.

When the school bell rang, the day was done.
Ruby red Schwoe took off in a run
To get away from the other children.

In the security of home with Mom and Dad
He told them of the horrible day he had.
They hugged their little ruby lad.

A plan was plotted for this little guy.
Mom and Dad knew what they had to try,
So they packed their bags and said, "Good bye."

The threesome left the land of Par-zee-no
Not exactly sure where to go.
Away, that's all they had to know.

The trip was long. The trek was hard.
They passed mountains and an old junkyard
Where a big, spotted dog stood on guard.

Through hail and fog and even some snow
They wandered, this family Schwoe,
Until they saw the brilliant rainbow.

Dad felt that the rainbow was a sign,
And knew everything would be just fine.
He led the family into warm sunshine.

Meanwhile, back in the
 land of Par-zee-no
There was a meeting of each
 and every Schwoe
Right after the family
 had decided to go.

Mayor Schwoe stood on a chair,
Looked across the crowd of purple hair,
And asked them all, "Don't you care?"

A hush fell across the crowd
And then a child spoke aloud,
"Of our actions, I am not proud."

One by one each Schwoe hung his head
Feeling sad and feeling dread
Because of the cruel things he'd said.

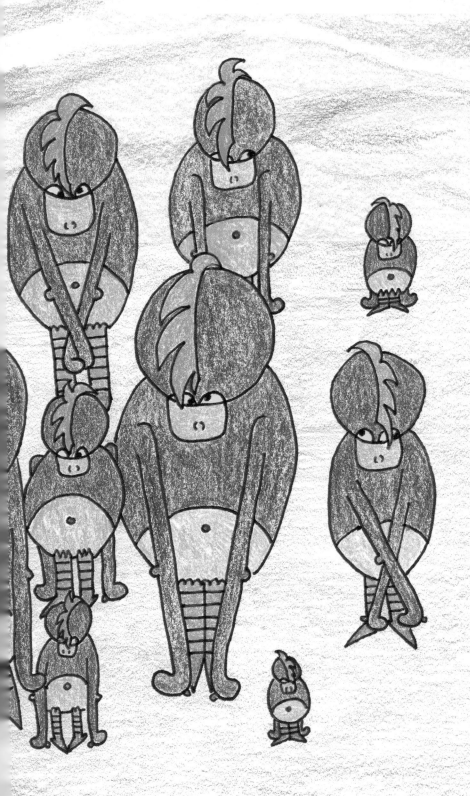

The Mayor once again addressed the Schwoes:
"We drove them off and where they are, who knows?
Perhaps we need help from the friendly crows."

The birds knew something was the matter
When they'd seen the crowd and heard the chatter.
They offered to help and so they scattered.

They soared toward the skies so blue
Knowing what they had to do –
Find Mom, Dad, and the red one, too.

Toward the end of the rainbow
Walked Mom, Dad, and little Schwoe.
They felt this was the way to go.

From far away the crows could see
The threesome, the wandering family.
They felt a sense of gleeful glee.

From the skies above they had a view.
The crows understood and knew
The rainbow would see the family through.

But the family plainly didn't know
Exactly where they would go.
They walked toward a grassy meadow.

The wise crows didn't say a thing.
They turned back and flapped each wing.
They had exciting news to bring.

You see, Mom and Dad and Ruby Schwoe
Were almost back to Par-zee-no.
That was the end of the rainbow.

The rest of the Schwoes had to prepare
To welcome them all, even red-hair,
And to show that they really did care.

They made a banner
 and held signs high
To welcome the family
 when they walked by,
And of course all
 had to apologize.

Imagine the family's
 shock and awe
When all three
 actually saw
They were home and not a single guffaw.

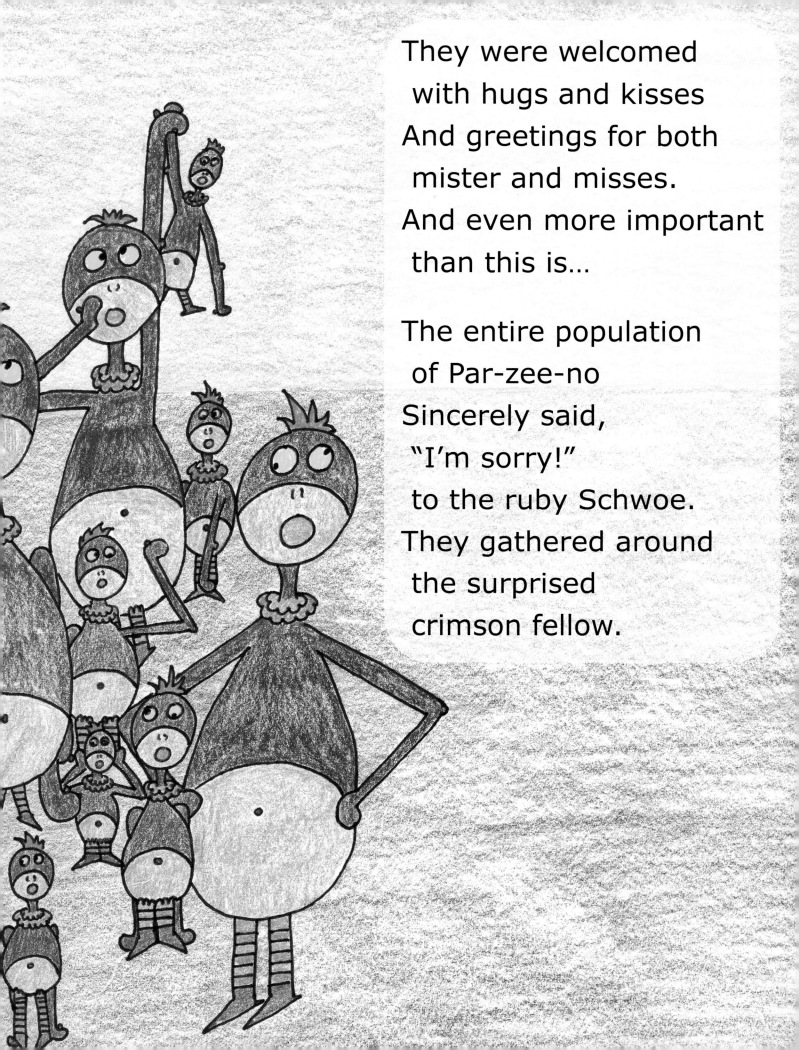

They were welcomed
 with hugs and kisses
And greetings for both
 mister and misses.
And even more important
 than this is…

The entire population
 of Par-zee-no
Sincerely said,
 "I'm sorry!"
 to the ruby Schwoe.
They gathered around
 the surprised
 crimson fellow.

"We were wrong.
We were badly bad.
We never thought
we'd made you sad.
But now you're back
and we are glad!"

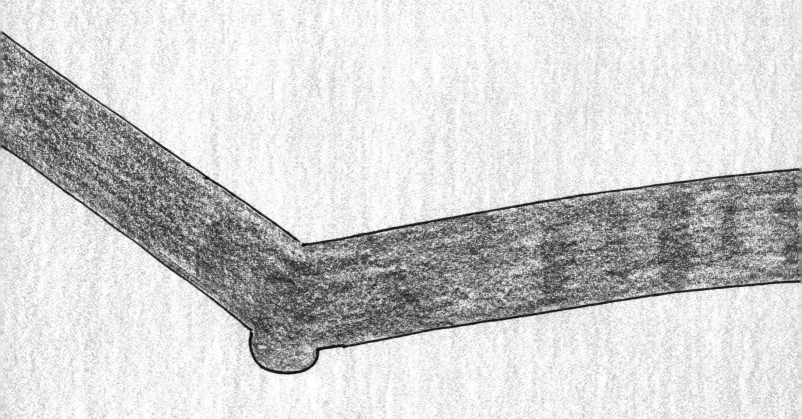

"Hip, hip, hooray!" they started to yell.
Somewhere someone rang a shiny bell,
And then a quiet quietness fell.

"It's great to be home. I'm pleased I'm here,"
The ruby-furred Schwoe said with great cheer.
"Thank you so much, friends, for coming here."

From that day on until forever
The Schwoes never judged someone, never.
They learned a lesson. Aren't they clever?

There's a message here for you to know:
Be just like a lovable Schwoe:
Embrace differences wherever you go.

Then you, too, will find the rainbow's end
Is not a pot of gold to spend
But the joy of being a loving friend.